CBeebies
BBC

**My Night-time
Treasury**

CBeebies
BBC

My Night-time Treasury

My Night-time Treasury

CONTENTS:

CONTENTS:

Tweenies™

Looking after Doodles

"Why can't Doodles get his own food?"
asked Fizz one day, when she and Bella and Milo
and Jake were watching Judy feed the dog.
"Because he can't put food into his own
bowl," said Judy. "Somebody has to do it for
him. Dogs need looking after."
"Just like children?"
asked Milo.

"Looking after a dog isn't the same
as looking after children," Judy explained.
"Oh, can we TRY to look after Doodles?" begged Bella.
"We can feed him and do things for him. Please?"
"All right," Judy agreed. "I'll be close by if you need any help."

13

The Tweenies took it in turns to look after Doodles. Fizz went first. She put ribbons in Doodles's hair to make him look pretty.

Then she put a nappy on him!

"Dogs don't wear nappies!" barked
Doodles.

"There's nothing to be ashamed of,"
Fizz insisted. "We've all
had to wear them."

When it was Milo's turn to look after Doodles,
he fastened a bib around his neck.
"Dogs don't wear bibs!" woofed Doodles.
"You have to keep your fur nice and clean," said Milo.

"Now, open wide – dinner time!" and he popped
a sandwich into Doodles's mouth.

16

Doodles didn't want the sandwich and he didn't want Milo's juice, either.

"Maybe you're not well," said Milo anxiously.

"Maybe I'm just not hungry," barked Doodles.

When it was Bella's turn to look after
Doodles, she said she'd take him for a walk.
Doodles raced to the door, barking loudly
and wagging his tail.

"WAIT!" ordered Bella. "First you have
to get dressed."

18

"But dogs don't wear clothes!" whined Doodles. Bella rummaged through the dressing up box.

"It's a nice sunny day," she said. "This shirt will be cool.

Sunglasses will keep the sun out of your eyes.

And a hat will stop your head from burning." At last Doodles was ready for his walk.

Milo followed Bella and Doodles into the garden.

"Doodles hasn't eaten his sandwich," he complained.

"Dogs don't eat sandwiches," said Bella. "They eat meat and bones."

"Where does Doodles keep his bones?" asked Milo.

"Dogs bury their bones," said Bella.

"Where do you bury your bones, Doodles?"

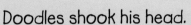

Doodles shook his head.

"I buried one in a very safe place," he barked. "But I just CAN'T remember where."

So Bella and Milo decided to sing Doodles a special song to help him.

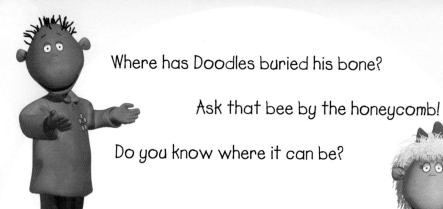

Where has Doodles buried his bone?

Ask that bee by the honeycomb!

Do you know where it can be?

Doodles's bone?
Don't ask me.
I've got honey
for my tea.

Don't want honey.
I want a bone!
Doodles wants a BONE!

22

Where has Doodles buried his bone?

Ask that cow there, all alone.

Do you know where it can be?

Doodles's bone?
Don't ask me.
I've got grass
for my tea!

Don't eat grass.
I want a bone.
Doodles wants a BONE!

23

Where has Doodles buried his bone?

Ask that bird. She's flown and flown.

Do you know where it can be?

Doodles's bone?
Don't ask me!
I've got worms
for my tea!

Don't want worms!
I want a bone!
Doodles wants a BONE!

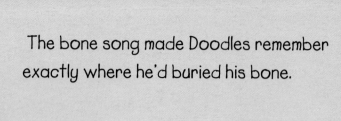

The bone song made Doodles remember exactly where he'd buried his bone.

He kept on digging

and digging

and digging

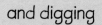

26

...until he found it
"Clever boy, Doodles," said Bella.
Then he heard someone calling him.
"Doodles, Doodles!" Doodles
pricked up his ears.
It was Jake he
scampered indoors.

27

Jake laughed when he saw Doodles.
"You look funny!" he teased.

Doodles barked and
chased Jake, and they
rolled together all over
the floor.

28

Bella and Fizz went to find Judy.

"Jake's messed up Doodles," they told her.

"I didn't mean to," cried Jake. "I was only playing with him. Anyway, Doodles looked silly in clothes!"

"No, he didn't!" said Bella. "He looked beautiful. And he was cool and dry and clean and everything."

30

"Jake's right," said Judy. "Dogs don't need to wear clothes. Doodles isn't like you or me. Doodles is a dog. He needs to be looked after just like a dog."

"Dogs need long walks, big bones, water, dog food and lots of love," said Judy.

"And dogs like to play," added Jake.

33

"Woof!" barked Doodles.
"That's what I like BEST!"

THE END

fimbles ™

Shoes

"One, two, three, four, five, once I caught a fish alive..." sang Fimbo. He was fishing in the Playdips.

"Glung! Bet you can't catch me!" giggled Rockit.

"Of course not! You're a frog, not a fish!" laughed Fimbo, as his nose started to twitch. "Oh! I'm getting the Fimbling Feeling! Perhaps I'll catch a fish."

Fimbo lifted up the rod and
found... a shoe on the end.

"It's not a fish, it's a shoe!" he
said. "I wish it was a fish! Perhaps
I'll go and show Pom the shoe,
and come back later to see if I've
caught anything."

"Fimbo? Pom? Rockit? Where are you?" called Florrie.

As Florrie and Little One walked towards the Playdips, Florrie's fingers began to twinkle.

"Oh! I'm getting the Fimbling Feeling!" she cried.

Florrie picked up Fimbo's fishing rod.

"It feels very heavy. I must have caught a fish!" she laughed. "One, two, three four, five, once I caught a fish alive..."

But all Florrie had caught was another shoe.

44

Fimbo came back with Baby Pom,
to see if he had caught a fish yet.
    "Look!" he said. "I found a shoe, too."
    "Fimbo, your shoe is the same as
mine!" cried Florrie.

"A pair of shoes!" said
Bessie.

"Shoes on! Shoes on!"
Baby Pom squealed. But the
shoes were too small for the
Fimbles' feet.

"Shoes are no fun," said
Fimbo. "I wanted a fish."

"Fimbo really wants to catch a fish," said Florrie to Baby Pom, at the Busy Base. "I know! Let's make a fish for Fimbo!"

Florrie got a piece of paper from the Busy Box, put the shoe on top, and drew around it with a pencil.

Then she cut the shape out. It looked like a fish.

"Shoe fish!" shouted Baby Pom. She and Florrie stuck an eye, scales and a tail onto the shoe fish.

53

"Maybe I should wish for a fish," Fimbo was saying to Rockit at the Playdips.

"Wissshhhh for a fissshhhh," chanted Rockit, waving his arms.

Fimbo was so busy watching Rockit, he didn't see Florrie slipping the shoe fish into the Playdips.

"Glung! Look on your fishing
line, Fimbo! You've caught a fish!"
shouted Rockit.

"I got my wish! I caught a
fish!" cried Fimbo.

"Shoe fish! Shoe fish!"
squealed Baby Pom, clapping
the shoes together. "Fish song!
Fish song!"

"Alright, Pom!" laughed Fimbo.

57

"One, two, three, four, five,
Once I caught a fish alive.
Six, seven, eight, nine, ten,
Then I let it go again.
Why did you let it go?
Because it bit my finger so!
Which finger did it bite?
This little finger on my right!"

1
2
3
4
5
6 7 8 9 10

Sleep Well, Teletubbies

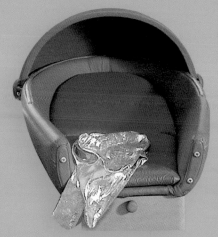

One day in Teletubbyland, all the
Teletubbies were feeling very, very tired.

Uh-oh!

60

So they decided to go to bed.

Ooooh!

Go to sleep, Teletubbies, go to sleep.
Go to sleep, Teletubbies, go to sleep.

62

There. All the Teletubbies are asleep.

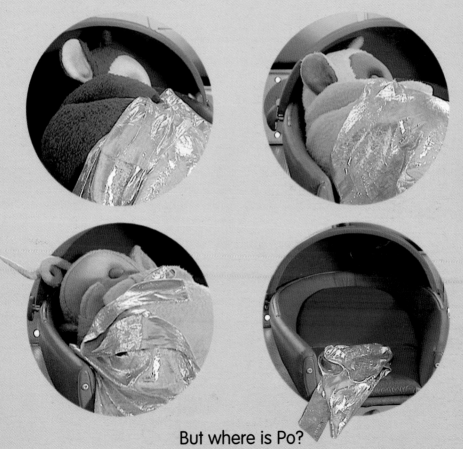

But where is Po?

Po is riding her scooter.

Scooter!

Uh-oh!

Po is **supposed** to be in bed.

Uh-oh!

Eh-oh!

Po is **supposed** to be in **bed!**

That's better.

Go to sleep, Teletubbies, go to sleep.
Go to sleep, Teletubbies, go to sleep.

66

Now all the Teletubbies are asleep.

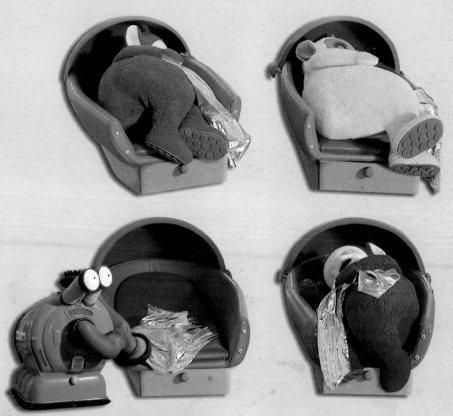

But where is Laa-Laa?

Laa-Laa is playing with her ball.

Uh-oh!

Laa-Laa is **supposed** to be in bed.

Uh-oh!

Laa-Laa is **supposed** to be in **bed!**

Eh-oh!

That's better.

Go to sleep, Teletubbies, go to sleep.
Go to sleep, Teletubbies, go to sleep.

All the Teletubbies **really are** asleep.

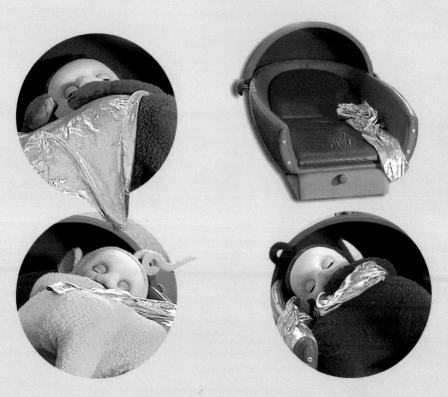

But where is Dipsy?

Dipsy has gone for a walk with his hat.

Dipsy is **supposed** to be in bed.

Uh-oh!

Dipsy is **supposed** to be in **bed!**

Eh-oh!

That's better.

Go to sleep, Teletubbies, go to sleep.
Go to sleep, Teletubbies, go to sleep.

74

All the Teletubbies are **definitely** asleep.

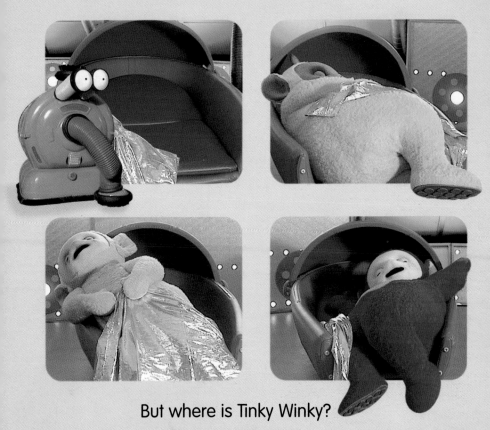

But where is Tinky Winky?

Tinky Winky is playing jumping with his bag.

Bag!

Uh-oh!

Tinky Winky is **supposed** to be in bed.

Uh-oh!

Tinky Winky is **supposed** to be in **bed**!

Eh-oh!

That's better.

Go to sleep, *Teletubbies*, go to sleep.
Go to sleep, *Teletubbies*, go to sleep.

Now all the Teletubbies **really are definitely** asleep.

79

Sleepy...snuffly...

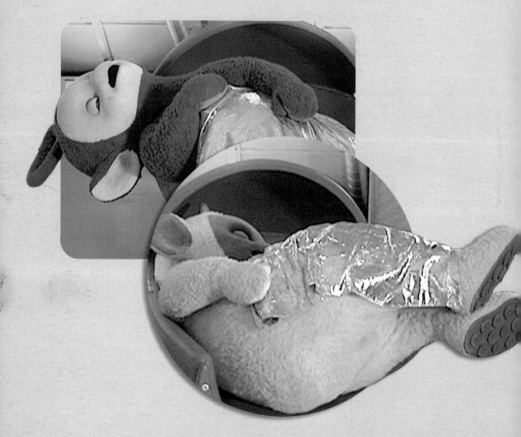

...snoozy...snore.

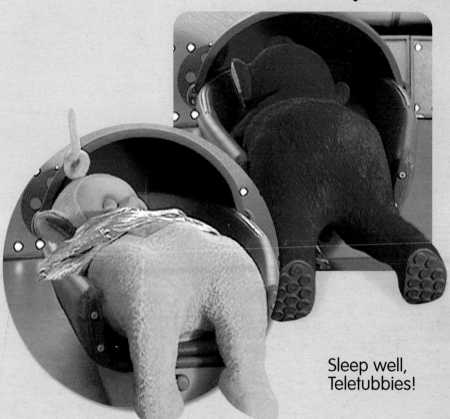

Sleep well,
Teletubbies!

Rock-A-Bye Robot

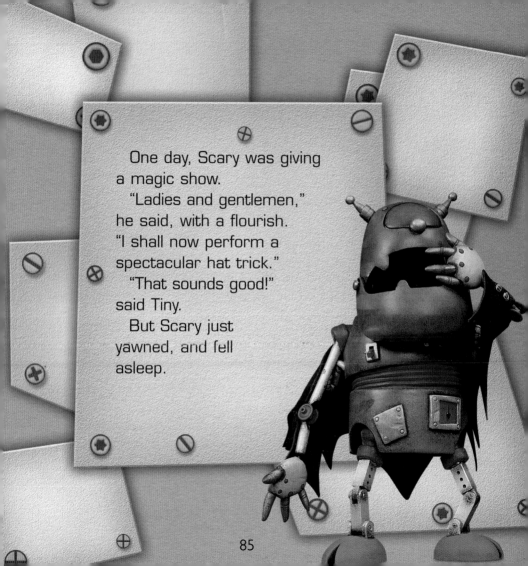

One day, Scary was giving a magic show.

"Ladies and gentlemen," he said, with a flourish. "I shall now perform a spectacular hat trick."

"That sounds good!" said Tiny.

But Scary just yawned, and fell asleep.

The robots looked
at each other in surprise.
Noisy laughed. "Scary's snoring!"

"Well, I haven't got time for this," said Stretchy, rolling off. "There's a delivery of junk due."

Tiny woke Scary. "Why are you so tired?" he asked.

Scary yawned.

"Sorry," he said. "I had a bad dream last night, and couldn't get back to sleep."

"Hmm," said Tiny.
"Why don't you sit down
on the stage and have a nap?
Noisy and I will think of
something to help you sleep
tonight."

"Let's build a rock-a-bye rocker!"
Tiny suggested.

"What's a rock-a-bye rocker?"
asked Noisy.

"It's a bed that plays a lullaby
and rocks you to sleep at the
same time," said Tiny. "I'll build
the rocker. You can make up
the lullaby on your xylophone."

While Tiny and Noisy
worked, Stretchy was waiting
for his next delivery.
Suddenly, the junk chute
began to rumble.

Thump! Something furry fell out.

"Goodness me, it's a teddy!" said Stretchy. "But he's not very well."

"I know someone who
likes teddies," thought Stretchy.
He went to see Stripy.
"Hello Stripy," said Stretchy.
"Can you mend this teddy?"

"I'll try," said Stripy,
gently holding the broken
teddy next to his own Teddy.
"I'll call him Fuzzy. Say hello to
Fuzzy, Teddy."

By the end of the day, Stripy
and Teddy had mended Fuzzy...

...and Tiny and Noisy had finished the rock-a-bye rocker.

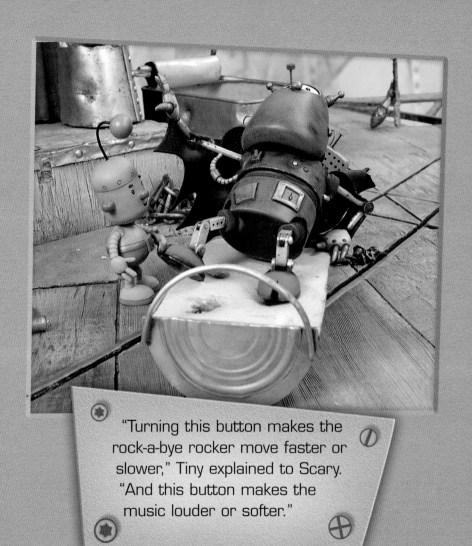

"Turning this button makes the
rock-a-bye rocker move faster or
slower," Tiny explained to Scary.
"And this button makes the
music louder or softer."

"Remarkable!" said Scary.
"Well, it's time for me to pull the Day-Night Lever," said Tiny.
"So you can try the rocker right away."

99

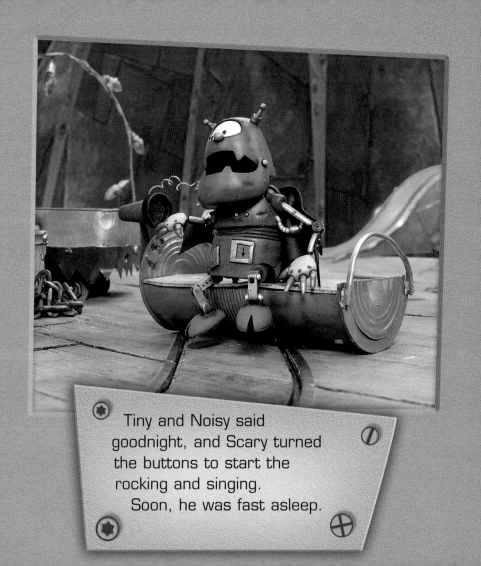

Tiny and Noisy said goodnight, and Scary turned the buttons to start the rocking and singing.

Soon, he was fast asleep.

But Flappy the bat
wasn't asleep.
    She wanted to play.
    She flew down and turned
one button. The music got louder.

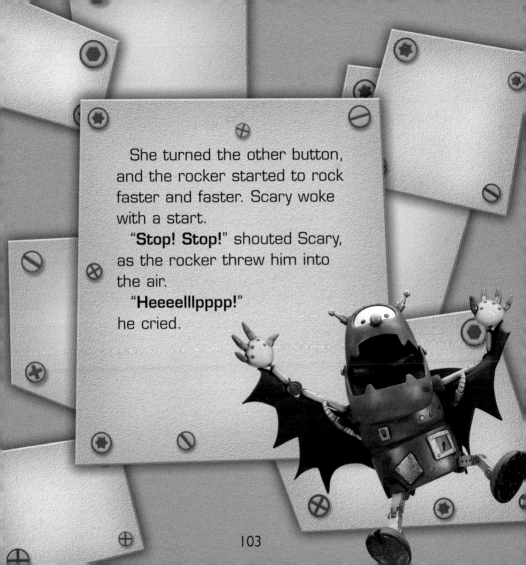

She turned the other button, and the rocker started to rock faster and faster. Scary woke with a start.

"**Stop! Stop!**" shouted Scary, as the rocker threw him into the air.

"**Heeeelllpppp!**" he cried.

Luckily for Scary, he
landed on Fuzzy.
"I say, Stripy!" said Scary.
"He's terrific. All soft and cuddly."
"He's called Fuzzy," said Stripy.

"Would you like to look after him? I already have Teddy."

Scary took Fuzzy home and stretched out to sleep on him. He slept soundly till morning.

But someone found a use for Tiny's rock-a-bye rocker. Flappy tied on some reins. Then she turned the rocking up fast, and played on the rocker all night long.

The End

the Rolymo Show!
fimbles

Sleepover

Little Bo's backpack felt much heavier than usual. As well as all her school things, it was full of everything she'd need for the night. She was going to her very first sleepover!

Little Bo had never slept at Uncle Roly's house before. She felt very grown-up.

"Hello there, Little Bo!" said Roly Mo, as she gave him a kiss. "I'm just getting the bed ready for..."

"My first sleepover!" said Little Bo.

Roly and Little Bo began unpacking her backpack at once. "Let's see," said Little Bo. "I've got my toothbrush, my toothpaste, my soap, my sponge..."

"...my Busy Book, and Floppy, of course," said Little Bo.

"You are organised," said Roly. "Anyone would think you'd been on a hundred sleepovers!"

Little Bo giggled proudly.

"Now, is there anything else we need?"
said Roly.

"Me!" said Yugo.

"And me!" said Migo.

"And last of all, a bedtime story,"
said Roly.

Sparkly White

Sparkly White

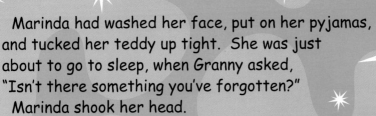

Marinda had washed her face, put on her pyjamas,
and tucked her teddy up tight. She was just
about to go to sleep, when Granny asked,
"Isn't there something you've forgotten?"
Marinda shook her head.
"Perhaps this will remind you," said Granny, and she sang:
"There's something you keep bright
By brushing every night,
And if you brush them right,
They'll stay all sparkly white."
Marinda gasped. "My teeth! I haven't brushed them yet!"

Granny sang the song again as Marinda brushed away.

"My granny used to sing that to me every night," said Granny. "I've never forgotten it."

"But I brush my teeth every morning too," said Marinda, climbing back under the covers.

Granny smiled. "Maybe tomorrow I'll teach you the morning rhyme."

Next morning, Marinda hurried back to the bathroom after breakfast.

"Quick, Granny, what's the morning rhyme?" she asked.

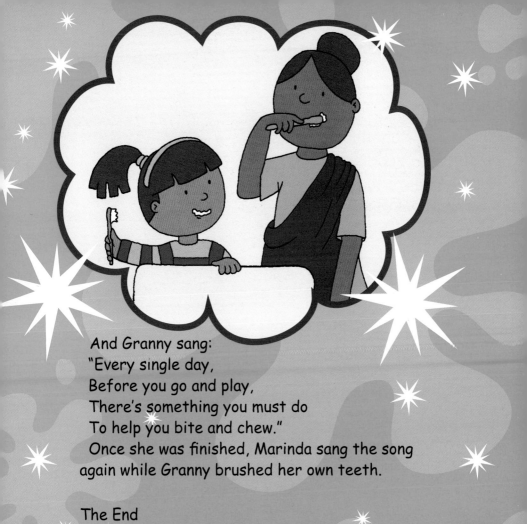

And Granny sang:
"Every single day,
Before you go and play,
There's something you must do
To help you bite and chew."
Once she was finished, Marinda sang the song
again while Granny brushed her own teeth.

The End

When Roly had
finished reading,
the snoots jumped
into their chest of
drawers with Snudge
and Bibby.

"Sleepytime!"
called Yugo.

"Time for beddy-
byes!" said Migo.

"Wait!" said Little Bo. "We've forgotten something. We haven't made our teeth sparkly white!"

Little Bo, Yugo and Migo brushed their teeth.
Then Roly tucked them in.

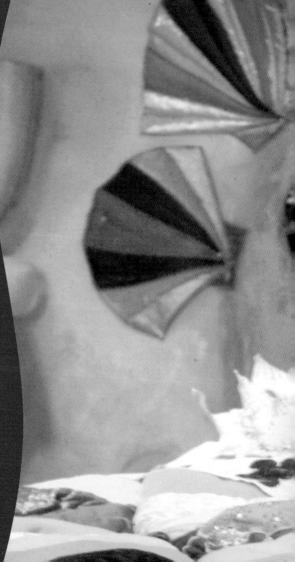

Little Bo lay there in the quiet. It felt strange to be sleeping in a different bed. She was very glad Floppy was with her.

Suddenly, a funny whistling noise made her jump. It was like nothing she'd ever heard before.

She jumped out of bed and ran down the corridor to the living room.

"Uncle Roly!" she cried. "I heard a funny noise!"
"Then why don't you stay here with me for a
little while," said Roly.

Roly made Little Bo a drink, and then Little Bo had a look through the Rolyscope. She could see hundreds of stars, twinkling in the dark blue sky.

125

"Now, shall we see what's making your funny noise?" said Roly.

Little Bo nodded. She kept close behind Roly as they tiptoed back to the bedroom.

Then she heard the noise again!

Roly laughed. "I know what that noise is! It's the snoots!"

Yugo and Migo were snootling away, fast asleep.

127

Little Bo laughed. Now she knew what it was, the noise didn't seem at all scary. In fact, it was nice knowing the snoots were so close. They could all play together in the morning.

She snuggled down in the bed, cuddling Floppy.
And before long, she was snootling too.

The End

Tweenies™
Brand New Choo-Choo!

Bella, Fizz and Milo were playing quietly indoors. But Jake wasn't joining in. He was wandering around the room looking upset.

"Have you seen my choo-choo?" he asked Fizz.

"No, sorry Jake. Have you lost it?" said Fizz.

Jake nodded.

"Would you like me to help you look for it?"

Jake nodded again.

So Fizz and Jake started to look around. They didn't find the train but they found Bella, sitting in the book corner.

"Have you seen my choo-choo?" asked Jake. "I've lost it."

"You mean your train, Jake? Where did you last play with it?"

Jake shrugged.

Bella sighed.

"Were you here in the book corner?"

"I don't think so, but I do like to bring my train over here and look at the pictures in the train book."

"Well, let's start here, then," Bella suggested.

Bella, Fizz and Jake looked
all around the book corner.
Fizz put her hand down
between two beanbags.

"I've found
something!" she called, and pulled up two coloured pencils.

136

Jake looked disappointed.

"You could draw a train with these," Fizz suggested.

"No, thank you," said Jake. "I want my train."

"What else do you do with your train, Jake?" asked Bella.

"I sometimes use the bricks to build a bridge for it," Jake replied.

So they went over to where
Milo was playing with the bricks.

"Milo, have you seen Jake's
train? He's lost it," said Fizz.

"No, but he can come and play
with the rocket launchpad I've
just built."

"No, thanks. I want my train,"
said Jake.

Fizz and Bella tipped
up the box of bricks
to see if Jake's train
was in there.

"Hey!" shouted Milo. "I've found the whistle from my Christmas cracker."

Milo started to toot very loudly.

"Let's go and look outside," shouted Bella.

Jake nodded.

"Sometimes I make hills and tunnels for my train in the sandpit."

There were quite a few
things in the sandpit —
buckets, spades, flags
and shells.

"Oh, look!" said Bella,
peering in. "I can see some
cotton reels. I think they
belong in the messy corner."

"But can you see my train,
Bella?" asked Jake.
Bella shook her head.
"Don't worry, Jake, there
are lots more places to try.
Let's take these in and look
in the messy corner."

Jake told them that he liked to run his train along the smooth worktop and stop at the paint pot stations. The Tweenies started to search.

"I can't see anything, Jake," said Fizz.

"Are you sure it could be here?"

Jake didn't answer.

Bella explained everything to Judy.
"And while we were looking for Jake's train, we found all these," said Fizz, laying everything on the table.

Judy gave Jake a hug and looked at what they had found.

"Don't worry, Jake. I've got an idea."

She found two boxes and a cardboard tube and stuck them together.

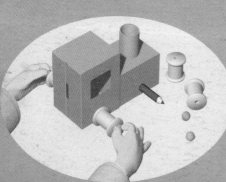

Then she poked the pencils through the boxes and put the cotton reels and little balls of modelling clay on the ends that stuck out.

Bella and Fizz painted the train bright red and decorated it with some gold stickers.

When they had finished, Jake was very pleased.

"A brand new choo-choo! Oh, thank you!"

"Toot Toot!" Milo grabbed the Christmas whistle and pretended to be a train. The others soon joined in, singing...

The wheels on the train go round and round,
round and round,
round and round.
The wheels on the train go round and round,
all day long.

The engine on the train goes
chuff, chuff, chuff,
    chuff, chuff, chuff,
        chuff, chuff, chuff.
The engine on the train goes
chuff, chuff, chuff,
    all day long.

The whistle on the train goes
toot, toot, toot,
    toot, toot, toot,
        toot, toot, toot.
The whistle on the train goes
toot, toot, toot,
    all day long.

The people in the train sway side to side,
  side to side,
    side to side.
The people in the train sway side to side,
                    all day long.

The wheels on the train go round and round,
round and round,
round and round.
The wheels on the train go round and round,
all day long.

The Tweenies ran around and around, faster and faster, and when they had run out of space indoors, they ran outside.

The Tweenie train
went up the slide.
Jake slid down first,
but stopped at the
bottom. The others
slid down after him.

"Hey!" said Jake.
"Sorry!" said
the others.

"No, look everyone!
Look what I've found!"
Jake laughed.

It was Jake's toy train.
"It wasn't lost at all!" said Fizz.
"It was just waiting at the station," said Bella.
"Toot! Toot!" said Milo.

Jake smiled. Now he had two choo-choos to play with!

THE END

BBC CHILDREN'S BOOKS
Published by the Penguin Group
Penguin Books Ltd, 80 Strand, London WC2R 0RL, England
Penguin Group (Australia), 250 Camberwell Road, Camberwell, Victoria 3124,
Australia (a division of Pearson Australia Group Pty Ltd)
Published by BBC Children's Character Books, 2007
Text and design © Children's Character Books, 2007
10 9 8 7 6 5 4 3 2 1
BBC & logo © and ™ BBC 1996
CBeebies & logo ™ BBC. © BBC 2002
ISBN 978 1 405 90395 0
Printed in China

Fimbles © and ™ BBC 2002. Fimbles is produced by Novel Entertainment for BBC/BBC
Worldwide Ltd. Licensed by BBC Worldwide Ltd.
'Shoes' first published in 2004 by BBC Worldwide Ltd. Adapted by Claire Sipi.
Based on the script by Rosemary Barratt.

Teletubbies characters and logo © and ™ 1996 Ragdoll Limited.
Licensed by BBC Worldwide Ltd.
'Sleep Well, Teletubbies' first published in 1998 by BBC Worldwide Ltd.
From original scripts by Andrew Davenport.